SACRAMENTO PUBLIC LIBRARY
828 "I" Street
Sacramento, CA 95814
08/19

D0099482

WITHDRAWN FROM COLLECTION
OF SACRAMENTO PUBLIC LIBRARY

the Itty-Bitty witch

Welcome,
1st Years!

by Trisha Speed Shaskan · illustrated by Xindi Yan

two lions

For my aunt Joette Gostomski, my favorite
Halloween Witchy Poo, for loving me every itty bit.
—T. S. S.

For my loving parents, without whom I would never
be able to live my dreams.
—X. Y.

Text copyright © 2019 by Trisha Speed Shaskan
Illustrations copyright © 2019 by Xindi Yan
All rights reserved.

No part of this book may be reproduced, or stored in a retrieval system, or
transmitted in any form or by any means, electronic, mechanical, photocopying,
recording, or otherwise, without express written permission of the publisher.

Published by Two Lions, New York
www.apub.com

Amazon, the Amazon logo, and Two Lions are trademarks
of Amazon.com, Inc., or its affiliates.

ISBN-13: 9781542041232
ISBN-10: 1542041236
The illustrations were created digitally.

Book design by Tanya Ross-Hughes
Printed in China

First Edition
10 9 8 7 6 5 4 3 2 1

Betty Ann Batsworth couldn't wait to get to her classroom.
It was her first day as a first-grade witch.

"Is that your kinder-broom?" Abby Owlsgate asked.
The other witches laughed. They had first-grade brooms.
"She isn't big enough for a real broom.
Let's call her Itty Bitty." Sam Catswell pointed.
"My name is Betty," Betty replied.
"Hi, Betty." Taylor Toadsley waved.

Between the broom closet and class,
other witches called Betty "Itty Bitty"
at least five times, which she didn't like.
Not one bit.
She started to feel itty-bitty inside.

During Morning Meeting, Ms. Fit said,
"This year you get to fly in
the Halloween Dash! Each grade
has its own race and
one winner. All month long,
we'll practice for it."

Halloween Dash

Betty had an idea.
If she won the Halloween Dash, maybe she
wouldn't be called Itty Bitty anymore!

The next day, Ms. Fit taught the witches to race.
The other witches bolted, but Betty's broom was shorter
and she couldn't keep up.

Betty had an idea.
What if she tried a running start?

SWOOSH!

WHOOSH!

UH-OH!

OOPS!

"Oh, Itty Bitty," Abby said.
And Betty felt itty-bitty inside.

For the whole month, the witches raced and chased.
Ms. Fit said, "Practice makes magic."

Betty tried for speed.
She nose-dived.

WHOOSH!

"Oh, Itty Bitty!" Sam said.
"It's Betty!" Betty said.
But she felt itty-bitty inside.

The next time Betty dreamed of speed, an idea flew by!

What if she flip-flapped her arms?

"Wicked!" Taylor said.

"Do you always have to be different?" Abby asked.

Finally, Ms. Fit showed the class the racecourse.
"Mind the cave and the trees. Stay on the path.
Ride the breeze."

How would Betty remember the way? Ms. Fit's words
gave her an idea. What if Betty made up a poem?

"Cattails, grave, pines, then cave,"
Betty said quietly.

"Weird!" Sam said. "Itty Bitty is talking to herself!"
Betty had had enough.
"It's BETTY!" she said.
But she still felt itty-bitty inside.

Halloween Dash

On the big day, the witches lined up
for the Halloween Dash.

"The first witch across
the finish line wins!" Ms. Fit said.

"On your mark! Get set! Fly!"

Betty got a running start. *SWOOSH!*

But her classmates soon caught up.
"Cattails, grave, pines, then cave," Betty said, steadying herself.

The witches raced toward the cave.

They flew up, down, and around it.

Betty s-l-o-w-e-d to do the same.

UH-OH!

She started to slide.

"See you and your kinder-broom later," Abby said.

Betty felt so itty-bitty, she thought she might
shrink small enough to disappear.

But that gave her the BIGGEST idea yet: What if
she became as itty-bitty as she could be?

SWOOSH!

Betty did what bigger witches couldn't do.
She flew straight through the cave!

"Wicked!" Taylor cheered.

As they raced to the finish line, Betty nose-dived.

"The winner is Betty!" Ms. Fit said.

"Itty Bitty?" Sam asked.

"No, **Itty BETTY!**" Betty said. She felt **BIG** inside.

The class chanted, "Itty Betty! Itty Betty!"
And Betty liked her new nickname.
Every itty bit.